THE Prince of

For Douglas ~ A.M.

To Eddie and Caroline ~ S.M.

First published in 2016 by Scholastic Children's Books
Euston House, 24 Eversholt Street, London NW1 1DB
a division of Scholastic Ltd

www.scholastic.co.uk

London ~ New York ~ Toronto ~ Sydney ~ Auckland ~ Mexico City ~ New Delhi ~ Hong Kong

Text copyright © 2016 Alan MacDonald • Illustrations copyright © 2016 Sarah McIntyre

HB ISBN 978 - 1407 - 15843 - 3
PB ISBN 978 - 1407 - 15844 - 0

Designed by Strawberrie Donnelly
Edited by Pauliina Malinen

PANTS

Alan MacDonald

Sarah McIntyre

SCHOLASTIC

Prince Pip jumped out of bed.
Today was his **birthday!**

Yippee!

Hooray!

"Now which **pants** shall I wear?" he thought.
Prince Pip had pants of **all kinds** - purple, gold,
starry, dotty, zebra stripes and leopard spotty.
He kept them all in a bottom drawer marked 'Pants'.

But which pants should he wear for his **birthday?**
Should it be his

morning pants

or his
evening pants?

He could wear his **pirate**
pants for an adventure...

or his **magician's** pants to play a trick.

He opened the drawer...

Pants

HELP! Oh bloomers! Oh NO!

Where were all his favourite pants? They must have **run off!**

There was **no time** to lose.

Prince Pip pulled on his boots and set out to look.

He couldn't have a birthday with **no pants!**

On the stairs he met the maid taking the Queen her breakfast.

"Have you seen my **pants?**" he asked.

"I think they've **run off!**"

The maid gave a giggle.

"Run off? Dearie dear, you'd better run after them then!"

Prince Pip rushed down the hall, almost bumping into the palace guards who were on duty.
"Have you seen my pants?" he begged. "Maybe they came this way."

The guards snapped smartly to attention.
"PANTS, SIR? NO SIR, NOT US, SIR!" they bellowed.

Prince Pip climbed the tower steps to find the king.

"Have you seen my pants, Daddy?" he puffed. "They've run off!"

The king chuckled.

"Run off, eh?"

Ha ha! Next you'll be saying they can fly!"

The Queen was out walking her dogs.

"Have **you** seen my pants, Mummy?" panted Pip. "They've **run off**, and I can't find them ANYWHERE!"

"Don't be a **noodle**, Pip!" said the Queen. "Pants cannot run. Look harder, my dumpling - they're probably right under your nose."

Prince Pip looked under his nose but his pants weren't there either. He wasn't having a happy birthday **at all**.

He dragged his feet back to the palace.
It was very quiet.

Where WAS everyone?

He opened a door...

"Happy Birthday!"

Prince Pip almost fell sideways in surprise. Everyone was in the ballroom and they were wearing pants!

His pants!

"It's a **Pants Birthday Party!**" announced the Queen. Prince Pip laughed. "So that's where all my pants had run off to!"

A present was pushed into his hands.

"Open it! Open it!"

everyone shouted.

Pip tore open the box.
"They're my favourite pants in all
the world!" he cried. "I'm never ever
taking them off! They're ..."

"...glow-in-
the-dark
pants!"

Hold this page under a bright light.
Then take the book to a dark room to see
Pip's pants *glow!*